LOVING TOUCHES

by
Lory Freeman

Illustrated by
Carol Deach

Parenting Press, Inc.
Seattle, Washington

Published by
Parenting Press, Inc.
P.O. Box 75267
Seattle, WA 98125

ISBN 0-943990-20-3 paper
ISBN 0-943990-21-1 library binding
LC 85-62434

Dedicated to my mom and dad who gave me loving touches when I needed them, and to Dylan, Sierra and David who helped make *Loving Touches* whole.

Introduction

Loving Touches is a reminder that truly loving touches are as necessary to human existence as food when we are hungry, and warmth when we are cold. This basic need remains with us throughout life. *Loving Touches* shows children positive ways to have this need met.

Children need a loving environment which both reinforces the importance of nurturing touches and teaches them to resist uncomfortable touch. We can do this by respecting children's feelings about who touches them and how.

It is helpful to integrate the child's personal experiences into the telling of *Loving Touches* in order to personalize the meaning of the story for the child. When reading the book, encourage the child to talk about his or her own personal experiences with positive touching and, of course, touching that they were uncomfortable with.

Loving Touches offers positive ways for children to get loving touches when they need them. Reinforce these concepts through discussion, positive feedback and adult modeling. Challenge the children to extend their perceptions beyond themselves to acknowledge other's needs to be touched or not to be touched.

The message of *Loving Touches* is for people of all ages. A healthy, productive life includes loving, human touch, which heals, soothes, nurtures and affirms the self.

When I was a baby I needed some very important things.

Did I need many, many kittens? No....

Did I need lots of big kid toys? No...

Or maybe a shiny, red tricycle? No...

I needed food when I was hungry...

Something to make me warm when I was cold...

And loving touches to make me feel just right!

I'm bigger now and I still need these three things.
I need food when I'm hungry...

8

I need something to make me warm when I'm cold...

And loving touches to make me feel just right!

Sometimes I need the hugging kind of loving touch.

When I want help, a lift-up can be a loving touch.

A tickle can be a loving touch, when I am having fun.

Sometimes, I need the "make it feel better" kind of loving touch.

A kiss can be a loving touch when I want one.

And some days, I need the sitting on the lap kind of loving touch.

When I need a loving touch, there are different ways I can ask for one. I can ask for a loving touch with my face...

Or I can ask for a loving touch with words like this:
"I need a hug."

18

Or I can give a loving touch and get one back.

When I'm older like my grandma and grandpa, I'll still need some very important things.

Will I need many, many kittens...lots of big kid toys...and a shiny new tricycle? No...

I'll need food when I'm hungry...

Something to make me warm when I'm cold...

And loving touches...to make me feel just right.

More Books to Help Protect Children

It's MY Body, by Lory Freeman and illustrated by Carol Deach, teaches children how to distinguish between "good" and "bad" touches, and how to respond appropriately to unwanted touches. Useful with 3-8 years, 32 pages, $5.95 paper, $15.95 library

Mi Cuerpo Es MIO, Spanish translation of *It's MY Body.* $5.95 paper

Protect Your Child from Sexual Abuse by Janie Hart Rossi offers parents information about sexual abuse and what to do to prevent child abuse. Useful with 1-12 years, 64 pages, $7.95 paper, $17.95 library

Loving Touches, by Lory Freeman and illustrated by Carol Deach, teaches children how to ask for and give positive and nurturing touches. Children also learn how to respect their own and other's bodies. Useful with 3-8 years, 32 pages, $5.95 paper, $15.95 library

Telling Isn't Tattling, by Kathryn Hammerseng and illustrated by Dave Garbot, helps children learn when to tell an adult they need help, and when to deal with problems themselves. Adults learn when to pay attention to kids' requests for help. Useful with 4-12 years, 32 pages, $5.95 paper, $15.95 library

The Trouble with Secrets, by Karen Johnsen and illustrated by Linda Johnson Forssell, shows children how to distinguish between hurtful secrets and good surprises. Useful with 3-8 years, 32 pages, $5.95 paper, $15.95 library

Something Happened and I'm Scared to Tell, by Patricia Kehoe, Ph.D. and illustrated by Carol Deach, is the story of a young sexual abuse victim who learns how to recover self-esteem. Useful with 3-7 years, 32 pages, $5.95 paper, $15.95 library

Helping Abused Children by Patricia Kehoe, Ph.D. provides many ideas and activities for care givers working with sexually abused children. Useful with 3-12 years, 48 pages, $10.95 paper, $18.95 library

Something Is Wrong at My House, by Diane Davis and illustrated by Marina Megale, offers children in violent homes ways to cope with the violence. Useful with 3-12 years, 40 pages, $5.95 paper, $15.95 library

Kids to the Rescue!, by Maribeth and Darwin Boelts and illustrated by Marina Megale, uses an interactive "what-would-you-do-if?" format, and prompts kids to think wisely in an emergency. Useful with 4-12 years, 72 pages, $7.95 paper, $17.95 library

Ask for these books at your favorite bookstore, or call toll free 1-800-992-6657. VISA and MasterCard accepted with phone orders. Complete book catalog available on request.

Prices subject to change without notice.